SPACE EXPLORATION
ROCKETS AND SPACE TRAVEL

by Walt K. Moon

BrightP✦int Press

San Diego, CA

© 2023 BrightPoint Press
an imprint of ReferencePoint Press, Inc.
Printed in the United States

For more information, contact:
BrightPoint Press
PO Box 27779
San Diego, CA 92198
www.BrightPointPress.com

ALL RIGHTS RESERVED.

No part of this work covered by the copyright hereon may be reproduced or used in any form or by any means—graphic, electronic, or mechanical, including photocopying, recording, taping, web distribution, or information storage retrieval systems—without the written permission of the publisher.

LIBRARY OF CONGRESS CATALOGING-IN-PUBLICATION DATA

Names: Moon, Walt K., author.
Title: Rockets and space travel / by Walt K. Moon.
Description: San Diego, CA: BrightPoint Press, [2023] | Series: Space exploration | Includes bibliographical references and index. | Audience: Grades 10-12.
Identifiers: LCCN 2022000174 (print) | LCCN 2022000175 (eBook) | ISBN 9781678204327 (hardcover) | ISBN 9781678204334 (eBook)
Subjects: LCSH: Rockets (Aeronautics)--Juvenile literature.
Classification: LCC TL782.5 .M59 2023 (print) | LCC TL782.5 (eBook) | DDC 621.43/56--dc23/eng/20220317
LC record available at https://lccn.loc.gov/2022000174
LC eBook record available at https://lccn.loc.gov/2022000175

CONTENTS

AT A GLANCE	4
INTRODUCTION LIFTOFF	6
CHAPTER ONE LEAVING EARTH	12
CHAPTER TWO REUSABLE ROCKETS	24
CHAPTER THREE TRAVELING IN SPACE	36
CHAPTER FOUR RETURNING FROM SPACE	48
Glossary	58
Source Notes	59
For Further Research	60
Index	62
Image Credits	63
About the Author	64

AT A GLANCE

- Rocket engines burn propellant to push a rocket off the ground and into space.

- Rockets are usually made up of multiple parts called stages. As the propellant in each stage is used up, the empty stage falls away. The rest of the rocket continues its journey.

- Engineers design rockets based on what is needed for a mission.

- In the past, most rockets were expendable. This means they could be used only once.

- Today, many companies are working on reusable rockets. These can land safely after being used. Then they can launch again.

- SpaceX's Falcon 9 has been a successful rocket that is partly reusable. The company's Starship is designed to be fully reusable.

- Spacecraft need a variety of systems to keep astronauts safe, navigate through space, and land at their destinations.

- Most spacecraft today use chemical rocket engines. In the future, ships may use nuclear thermal propulsion (NTP).

- Spacecraft use equipment such as heat shields, parachutes, and rocket engines to land safely on planets and moons.

INTRODUCTION

LIFTOFF

It's a bright summer day on the Texas coast. A rocket towers almost 400 feet (122 m) above the sandy landscape. Its steel skin gleams under the midday sun. Twelve astronauts wait inside the ship. A few miles away, the control center is buzzing with activity. The countdown has begun.

Suddenly, the rocket roars to life. More than thirty engines light up, and a loud crackling sound fills the air. The rocket begins moving upward. Its many engines leave a long, bright trail of flame

SpaceX hopes to design rockets that can travel to deep space.

behind them. The rocket speeds up and begins tilting to one side.

A few minutes into the flight, the rocket is many miles high. It's going thousands of miles per hour. Then the engines go silent. The rocket splits into two parts called stages. The second stage is the front part. It has six engines of its own. These engines fire, boosting the ship into space. The rocket's first stage begins a long fall back to Earth. Computers in the rocket will steer and land it. Then it can be used again.

The crew members have had a thrilling ride to space. But their mission is just

It takes a lot of power to launch a rocket into space.

beginning. Next, they will meet up with another spacecraft. This ship carries **propellant**. It will refill their own ship's tanks. This will give them enough fuel to reach Jupiter. They hope to learn more about the beautiful planet and its moons.

ROCKETING INTO THE FUTURE

The first rocket to reach **orbit** around Earth launched in 1957. The first human spaceflight came four years later. In 1969, humans first walked on the Moon. The powerful Saturn V rocket took them there. A journey to Jupiter may be possible someday. So far, humans have sent only probes to the planet.

Technology has come a long way since the early days of space travel. Rockets once crashed into the land or sea after each flight. A new one was built for each mission. Now, some rockets can land and be

Astronaut Buzz Aldrin walked on the Moon after a successful flight on the Saturn V rocket.

reused. This will make space travel cheaper and more common. The rockets of the future will let people visit Mars, Jupiter, and other destinations in our solar system.

1
LEAVING EARTH

People use rockets to leave Earth and get into space. A rocket is a vehicle that burns propellant to push itself forward. Propellant includes two separate parts. The first is fuel. The second is **oxidizer**. Together, these two materials burn violently. The resulting flames and gas shoot out of the rocket engine. This pushes the vehicle forward.

Getting into space is challenging. Rockets must reach an amazingly high

Rockets burn propellant to provide power to get into space.

speed. This requires powerful engines and a lot of propellant. But that makes the rocket large and heavy. It's difficult to launch a large, heavy object into space.

One way to solve this problem is to divide the rocket into multiple parts called stages. Each stage has its own engines and propellant tanks. The first stage launches the rocket off the ground. As the rocket rises, it uses up its propellant and becomes lighter. This causes it to accelerate faster and faster. When the first stage runs out of fuel, it falls away. Acceleration stops for a moment. Then the second stage starts its

NASA successfully launched a four-stage rocket over Alaska in 2015. Fire from each stage is visible in this time-lapse photo.

engines. Without the first stage, the vehicle is smaller and lighter. It becomes easier to reach space.

Most rockets have two or three stages. The crew sits in the second stage of some reusable rocket designs. In other designs, the crew sits in a spacecraft that is separate from the stages.

DESIGNING AND BUILDING ROCKETS

Before a rocket can be launched, it must be designed and built. This process can take years. The first step in designing a rocket

ORBITAL VS. SUBORBITAL

Some rockets travel straight up into space. Then they come straight back down. This is known as a suborbital flight. Other rockets travel upward and also sideways. They gain enough sideways speed to go into orbit. This is an orbital flight. An orbital flight takes about 30 times as much energy as a suborbital one. This means a much larger rocket is needed.

is to figure out what it will be used for. A rocket's size depends on the **payload** it needs to carry. Some rockets launch small **satellites**. Others carry a few people to space stations. A larger rocket can carry more mass. It can also travel farther. Designers must pick the best size for the mission.

Rocket designers select engines and propellants. Some rockets use a few large engines. For example, the Saturn V used five gigantic F-1 engines. The Falcon Heavy, built by the company SpaceX, uses twenty-seven smaller Merlin engines.

Space companies hope to develop rockets that can travel to Mars.

Each engine uses a specific set of propellants. The F-1 and Merlin both use a fuel called RP-1. They use liquid oxygen as the oxidizer. Some newer engines use liquid methane as fuel. SpaceX's Raptor engine is one of them. The BE-4 engine, built by the company Blue Origin, is another.

One benefit of methane is that it can be produced on Mars. Future missions to the Red Planet could make their own fuel. They wouldn't need to carry fuel with them for the return journey. This could make it easier to launch back to Earth.

A rocket launch involves more than just the rocket itself. Ground equipment is needed as well. Support structures hold the rocket in place. Tanks of propellant are needed to fuel the rocket. An access arm extends from the support structure to let the crew board the rocket.

In the future, ground equipment may do even more. SpaceX plans for its Super Heavy rocket to land back on the launch pad. Huge arms will catch the booster. This will make reusing the rocket easier and quicker for future travel. Many companies are rethinking their launch equipment to make space missions cheaper and more frequent.

Transporting large rockets to launch pads can be difficult. The company Astra has designed a rocket that can be loaded into a

NASA built large rocket stages as part of its Artemis mission. In 2020, the 212-foot (65-m) stage was the largest NASA had ever built.

normal shipping container. This will make it cheaper to get rockets to launch sites.

TIME FOR LAUNCH

Astronauts are not the only people involved during a rocket launch. Ground crews check the rocket before launch. They keep an eye on the weather. High winds or lightning could make a launch unsafe. The rocket's computers send information about its condition. Workers at a launch control center monitor this data. They may cancel the launch if there is a problem.

ABORT

Rockets that carry people are carefully designed and checked. But accidents still happen. Something could go wrong with the rocket during launch. This is why many rockets have abort systems. These systems let the crew escape. They often use small rocket engines to yank the spacecraft to safety. Then the spacecraft can use parachutes to land.

If everything looks good, the countdown to launch begins.

Riding in a rocket is a thrilling experience. Astronaut Shane Kimbrough rode a Falcon 9 rocket in 2021. He said:

The first stage was, I would say, fairly smooth. . . . [Then] we got to experience that [second-stage] engine lighting, and then kind of a little [push] back in our seats and then pure acceleration for the next six-and-a-half minutes or so. It was a bit rumbly, it kind of was like . . . being on a rocky road in a vehicle.[1]

2
REUSABLE ROCKETS

For decades, almost all rockets could be used only once. These are called expendable rockets. After rocket stages used up their propellant, they fell into the ocean. Hitting the water at high speeds destroyed them. Expendable rockets work well, but launching them is expensive. A new rocket must be built each time.

Today, some rocket stages can be reused. This can bring down costs. For example, the Delta IV Heavy is a powerful

A recovery ship collects the SpaceX Crew Dragon Endeavour spacecraft. SpaceX hopes to make this spacecraft partially reusable.

expendable rocket. Each launch costs about $350 million. The Falcon Heavy has similar power. But its first stage is reusable. Each launch costs around $90 million. Cheaper launches may make space travel more common in the future.

THE SPACE SHUTTLE

The Space Shuttle was used between 1981 and 2011. It was a partly reusable spacecraft. It was made up of a spacecraft called the orbiter, a large orange propellant tank, and a pair of white rocket boosters. The orbiter could glide back to Earth and land like an airplane. The boosters landed with parachutes and could be reused. But after each flight, the propellant tank dropped into the sea and was destroyed.

THE FALCON 9

SpaceX started testing its Falcon 9 rocket in 2010. It was a medium-sized expendable rocket. The rocket carried satellites into space. It also brought supplies to the International Space Station (ISS). SpaceX studied how it could make the Falcon 9 reusable.

In 2014, the company began trying to land the rocket's first stage. It was a challenging task. The stages separate before the first stage runs out of propellant. The second stage continues to space. The first stage flips around and fires its engines to slow down. Grid-shaped fins steer the stage as it falls down to Earth. At the last moment, landing legs extend and the engines fire again. The stage comes in for a soft landing near the launch pad or on a ship at sea.

It took time for this plan to work. Several tests ended in explosions. Rockets blew up in the air or crashed into the sea. But each failure taught the engineers new lessons. They made improvements. The first successful landing happened in December 2015. In 2021, the company landed its ninetieth rocket.

SpaceX prepared to launch a Falcon 9 rocket in October 2021.

Elon Musk is the head of SpaceX. After the company landed its first reused rocket, he explained why reusing rockets is important. He said, "It's the difference between having airplanes that you threw away after every flight, versus reusing them multiple times."[2]

The Falcon 9 is not fully reusable. Only the first stage returns safely to Earth. The second stage burns up in the **atmosphere** after it is used. Reusing a second stage is difficult. The second stage is traveling much

LEARNING FROM FAILURE

In 2017, SpaceX released a video called "How Not to Land an Orbital Rocket Booster." It showed many of the explosions during Falcon 9 testing. The video's music was a marching band song, and the on-screen text poked fun at the company. The video ended with the company's first successful landing. By 2022, the video had racked up more than 27 million views.

faster by the time its job is done. It needs a heat shield to survive reentry. This is when a spacecraft reenters Earth's atmosphere.

STARSHIP AND BEYOND

A fully reusable rocket could make space travel cheaper and easier. The entire rocket could be used multiple times. This is the goal of SpaceX's Starship.

Starship has two stages. The first stage is called Super Heavy. It has more than thirty of the company's Raptor engines. It stands 230 feet (70 m) tall and is 30 feet (9.1 m) across. It works similarly to the first

Many current rocket designs, such as SpaceX's Starship, include several stages that can break away and be reused.

stage of the Falcon 9. After the stages separate, it uses its engines to fly back to the launch pad. Grid fins help it steer to a safe landing.

The second stage shares its name with the combined rocket. It is also called

Starship. This stage is 160 feet (50 m) long. It has shiny steel skin and moveable fins at the front and back. Six Raptor engines push Starship into space. It can meet another ship in orbit to refill its propellant tanks. Then it can travel to other places in the solar system.

    The Starship second stage uses a heat shield to protect against the intense temperatures of reentry. Then, it falls through the atmosphere on its belly. It uses its fins to steer, just like a skydiver using her arms as she falls. Falling like this slows the ship down. When it nears the ground,

A STARSHIP MISSION

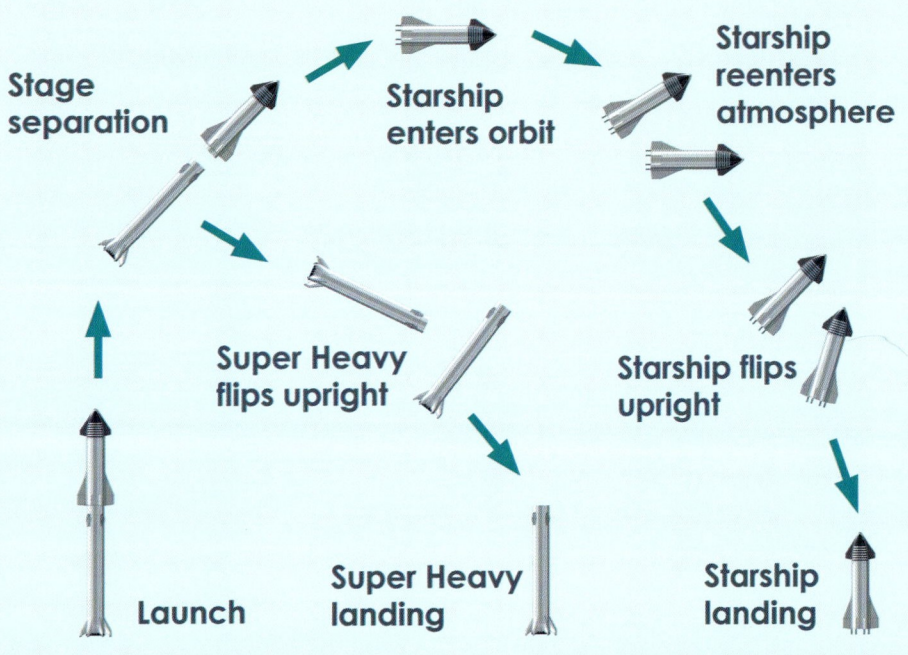

SpaceX's goal is to rapidly reuse Starship and Super Heavy.

Starship lights a few of its engines. The engines swing the stage upright. Then Starship comes to rest on its small landing legs. It can be refueled and flown again.

SpaceX first tested the Starship second stage in December 2020. Starship launched a few miles high, then shut off its engines. It tilted over on its side and steered using its fins. Then it tested using its engines to flip upright and land. The first Starship landed too hard and blew up. A few more tests also ended in explosions. But each time, the company learned more. In May 2021, a Starship landed successfully for the first time. The company next planned to test Super Heavy and Starship together. Many more tests are needed before people can ride Starship to space.

3
TRAVELING IN SPACE

Building a spacecraft is challenging. These vehicles need to be tough to survive in a harsh environment. But they also need to be as light as possible in order to launch. Spacecraft need to be reliable too. If they carry people, one serious problem could doom the crew. Engineers have found many ways to accomplish these goals.

Spacecraft come in many shapes and sizes. But most have a few basic systems

Rocket stages can be very large. Many people work on each stage to make sure that it functions correctly.

in common. They need electrical power to run computers and other equipment. They need communications gear to talk to people back on Earth. A **propulsion** system uses engines to speed up or slow down. Smaller engines point the ship in new directions.

POWER

Spacecraft can generate electrical power in many ways. Solar power turns sunlight into electricity. Radioisotope thermoelectric generators are another option. These devices collect heat from radioactive materials. This heat can be turned into electricity. Some missions use devices called fuel cells. Fuel cells mix oxygen and hydrogen to form water. This chemical reaction generates electricity.

Spacecraft use navigation systems to figure out where they are and where they're going. Life support equipment keeps the humans onboard alive. Finally, the spacecraft's structure holds everything together.

As of 2022, spacecraft had carried humans as far as the Moon. Getting there took about three days. In the future, people will travel to Mars and beyond. These journeys will take months or even years. New spacecraft technology will be needed to make this possible.

GETTING AROUND

Flying in space is different from flying in an atmosphere. Airplanes must be shaped to fly through the air smoothly. But space is a vacuum. There is no air. This means spacecraft can have odd shapes. The lunar module was used to land on the Moon. It looked a bit like a large bug. It had long legs, strange bulges, and sharp angles. It would never work on Earth. But if a spacecraft is used only in space, it doesn't matter what its shape is.

A spacecraft's propulsion system lets it change its speed. This lets a ship leave orbit

Spacecraft such as the lunar module may have strange shapes.

around Earth. Then it can travel to another planet. Today's ships mostly use chemical rocket engines for this. These engines burn propellants to create **thrust**. They work the same way as the rockets that launched the ship from Earth.

Chemical rocket engines work well. They have carried people to the Moon. They have launched robotic spacecraft to distant worlds. But future spacecraft may use different technology. Scientists are studying nuclear thermal propulsion (NTP). This system splits atoms to make heat. The heat burns propellant, pushing the spacecraft forward.

NTP creates less thrust than chemical rockets. This means it would not be useful for launching from Earth. But the thrust lasts longer. This means a spacecraft using NTP can reach a higher speed than a chemical rocket using the same amount of fuel. NTP may be useful once the ship is already in space. It can take nine months to reach Mars using a chemical rocket. Experts think NTP could cut that time to three months.

NTP HISTORY

NASA scientists first studied NTP in the 1960s. They hoped to use the engines to send astronauts to Mars. The scientists built and tested engines on the ground, but they never tried NTP in space. NASA decided not to plan a Mars mission, and the program ended in 1972. Modern scientists have picked up where early researchers left off.

Jeff Sheehy studies space technology at NASA. He explains that a faster trip is a safer trip. He says, "The longer you're out there, the more time there is for stuff to go wrong."[3]

SURVIVING SPACE

Many of the dangers of space come from being in a vacuum. A spacecraft must hold air pressure to keep the crew alive. It needs to provide oxygen to breathe. It must not get too hot or too cold. Another danger comes from an invisible form of energy called radiation. Radiation can damage a

The material that makes up spacecraft and spacesuits protects astronauts from the extreme conditions of space.

person's cells. This can increase the risk of cancer.

Earth has a powerful magnetic field. It blocks radiation from the Sun. This keeps people on Earth safe. The magnetic field extends into space. This means people in orbit around Earth are protected too. But people traveling farther away leave this area of protection. This is a concern for future missions.

Sometimes the Sun gives off bursts of radiation called solar storms. Astronauts will need to take cover. They can set up a temporary radiation shelter in their ship. They could surround themselves with food and water containers. Any material can help block some radiation. Space scientist Kerry Lee explains why a shelter might be made using these storage containers.

Solar storms create radiation that can be harmful to astronauts.

He says, "It's unlikely that we're going to be able to [pack] dedicated radiation-shielding mass. Every item you fly will have to be multi-purpose."[4] This would save weight compared to carrying a separate shelter.

4
RETURNING FROM SPACE

Spacecraft must reach high speeds to escape the gravity of the planet they launched from. They continue moving quickly to reach their destinations. Traveling fast means voyages take as little time as possible.

However, high speeds also create a problem. Spacecraft need to slow down to land safely. Engineers have found ways to achieve this. They study how future spacecraft will manage this tricky task.

A rocket needs to travel approximately 25,000 miles per hour (40,000 kmh) to leave Earth.

ENTRY

Some places, such as Earth and Mars, have atmospheres. This band of air helps slow the spacecraft down. But moving through the atmosphere at high speeds compresses air in front of the ship. This creates extreme heat. The spacecraft needs

SPACE ELEVATOR

One futuristic idea for going to space is called a space elevator. A huge cable would be anchored to the ground. It would extend all the way up into space. Vehicles could simply climb up the cable into orbit. Today's materials are not strong enough to build a space elevator. But scientists are studying how to make a space elevator possible in the future.

A reentering spacecraft experiences high heat and extreme forces.

a heat shield to protect itself. In the Apollo program of the 1960s, spacecraft returned from the Moon. Temperatures reached about 5,400 degrees Fahrenheit (3,000°C) during reentry. The spacecraft needed heavy heat shields.

Astronaut Scott Horowitz flew to space four times. He described what reentry was like. Horowitz said:

You'll notice, looking out the window, the sky starts to turn a different color. It turns kind of a light pinkish color, and then it gets kind of a deeper pinkish red, and then it turns red and orange. And what you realize is you're looking from the inside of a fireball outward.[5]

Other places, such as the Moon, don't have an atmosphere. This means air can't help the spacecraft slow down. It must use rocket engines to create thrust in the opposite direction to slow down.

TOUCHDOWN

After losing most of its speed during entry, a spacecraft needs to make a soft landing. On planets with thick atmospheres, a parachute can be used. It slows the

AEROBRAKING

Spacecraft often arrive at a planet going at high speeds. They can use the planet's atmosphere to slow down without landing. This is called aerobraking. A ship can dip into the atmosphere just enough for air to slow it down. It can enter a stable orbit around the planet. Using aerobraking instead of using the engines to slow down can save fuel.

spacecraft's fall. On Earth, the ship can splash into the ocean or touch down on dry land. Parachutes don't work in places without an atmosphere. Spacecraft must use their engines all the way to the ground.

Places with a thin atmosphere, such as Mars, are especially tricky. The atmosphere is thick enough that a ship needs a heat shield. However, it is too thin to use a parachute for landing. Parachutes only slow the spacecraft down a little. Rockets must be used at the end to make a soft landing.

SpaceX plans to land Starship on Mars. It will work the same way as on Earth. A heat

Parachutes can help slow spacecraft down as they reenter Earth's atmosphere.

shield will protect it during entry. Then it will fall through Mars's atmosphere on its belly. Just before landing, its engines will fire. Starship will flip upright and land.

A FUTURE IN SPACE

The world of rockets and space travel is exciting. Engineers are designing new vehicles for new missions. SpaceX has its Starship. Blue Origin plans to build a huge reusable rocket called New Glenn. Many other companies are building their own rockets, large and small.

The people behind these rockets have big dreams. Jeff Bezos is the head of Blue Origin. He wants to build huge space stations so people can live in space. Bezos says, "These are very large structures, miles on end, and they hold a million people or

Scientists continue to improve reusable rockets. These rockets will someday be used to travel to Mars and beyond.

more each."[6] Plans like these are many years away. But today's cutting-edge rockets and spacecraft are taking the first steps.

GLOSSARY

atmosphere

the layer of gas surrounding a planet or moon

orbit

a round path that an object takes when traveling around another object in space

oxidizer

a substance that releases oxygen, allowing fuel to burn in a rocket engine

payload

something carried by a rocket into space, such as a satellite or spacecraft

propellant

the chemicals, including a fuel and an oxidizer, that a spacecraft's engines use

propulsion

the action of pushing something forward

satellites

robotic spacecraft launched into orbit around a planet or moon

thrust

the pushing force created by a rocket engine

SOURCE NOTES

CHAPTER ONE: LEAVING EARTH

1. Quoted in William Harwood, "Astronauts Describe Thrilling Ride to Orbit on Falcon 9 Rocket," *Spaceflight Now*, April 30, 2021. https://spaceflightnow.com.

CHAPTER TWO: REUSABLE ROCKETS

2. Quoted in April Glaser, "SpaceX Just Made History by Successfully Reusing a Rocket," *Vox*, March 30, 2017. www.vox.com.

CHAPTER THREE: TRAVELING IN SPACE

3. Quoted in Nell Lewis, "Nuclear-Powered Rocket Could Get Astronauts to Mars Faster," *CNN*, February 10, 2021. www.cnn.com.

4. Quoted in Lina Tran, "How NASA Will Protect Astronauts from Space Radiation at the Moon," *NASA*, August 7, 2019. www.nasa.gov.

CHAPTER FOUR: RETURNING FROM SPACE

5. Quoted in "The Return from Space," *NPR*, August 7, 2005. www.npr.org.

6. Quoted in Corey S. Powell, "Jeff Bezos Foresees a Trillion People Living in Millions of Space Colonies. Here's What He's Doing to Get the Ball Rolling," *NBC*, May 15, 2019. www.nbcnews.com.

FOR FURTHER RESEARCH

BOOKS

Aiyanna Milligan, *Cutting-Edge SpaceX News*. Minneapolis, MN: Lerner Publishing, 2020.

Rachael L. Thomas, *Wernher von Braun: Revolutionary Rocket Engineer*. Minneapolis, MN: Abdo Publishing, 2019.

Philip Wolny, *Living in Space*. San Diego, CA: BrightPoint Press, 2023.

INTERNET SOURCES

"How Do Spacecraft Manoeuvre in the Vacuum of Space?" *Guardian*, February 7, 2021. www.theguardian.com.

Paul Rincon, "What Is Elon Musk's Starship?" *BBC News*, August 7, 2021. www.bbc.com.

"What Is a Rocket?" *NASA*, July 13, 2011. www.nasa.gov.

WEBSITES

NASA
www.nasa.gov

The official website of NASA features information about the latest space missions and the rockets and spacecraft that will be used to accomplish them.

Smithsonian National Air and Space Museum: How Things Fly
https://howthingsfly.si.edu

This website from the National Air and Space Museum has information, photos, and videos showing how rockets work and how spacecraft move around in space.

SpaceX
www.spacex.com

SpaceX's official website includes information about the company's rockets and spacecraft, including the Falcon 9, Dragon, and Starship.

INDEX

atmosphere, 30, 33, 34, 40, 50, 52–55

Bezos, Jeff, 56
Blue Origin, 19, 56

computers, 8, 22, 38

Delta IV Heavy, 25–26

engines, 7–8, 13–15, 17–18, 22, 23, 27–28, 38, 43, 53–55
    BE-4, 19
    chemical rocket engines, 41–43
    F-1, 17–18
    Merlin, 17–18
    Raptor, 18, 31–35
expendable rockets, 24–27

Falcon 9, 23, 27–30, 32
Falcon Heavy, 17, 26
fuel, 9, 12, 14, 18–19, 38, 43, 53

heat shields, 31, 33, 51–52, 54

launch pad, 20, 28, 32

Mars, 11, 19, 39, 43, 50, 54–55
methane, 18–19
Musk, Elon, 29

nuclear thermal propulsion (NTP), 42–43

oxidizers, 12, 18

parachutes, 22, 26, 53–54
payloads, 17
power, 26, 38
propellants, 9, 12, 14, 17–19, 24, 26, 27, 33, 41–42

radiation, 44–47
reentry, 31, 33, 34, 51–52
reusable rockets, 11, 16, 20, 25–35, 56

satellites, 17, 27
SpaceX, 17–18, 20, 27, 29–31, 34–35, 54, 56
stages, 8, 14–16, 23, 24–28, 30–35
Starship, 31, 33–35, 54–56
Super Heavy, 20, 31, 34, 35

IMAGE CREDITS

Cover: Terry White/SLS/MSFC/NASA
5: KSC/NASA
7: © Paopano/Shutterstock Images
9: © 3D Sculptor/Shutterstock Images
11: JSC/NASA
13: © Elen11/iStockphoto
15: Jamie Adkins/NASA Goddard/GSFC/NASA
18: © Josh I. Merbin/Shutterstock Images
21: Danny Nowlin/MAF/NASA
25: Bill Ingalls/HQ/NASA
29: SpaceX/KSC/NASA
32: Official SpaceX Photos/Flickr
34: © David Lugasi/Shutterstock Images
37: Glenn Benson/KSC/NASA
41: NASA/Wikipedia
45: SpaceX/KSC/NASA
47: NASA Goddard/GSFC/NASA
49: Trevor Mahlmann/Rocket Lab/KSC/NASA
51: © Marc Ward/Shutterstock Images
55: Bill Ingalls/HQ/NASA
57: © Paopano/Shutterstock Images

ABOUT THE AUTHOR

Walt K. Moon lives in Minnesota. He enjoys reading and writing about the past, present, and future of rockets and space travel.